Ashok Rajagopalan's main aim in life is to make people, especially little people, laugh. He has been doing this since 1989, by writing and illustrating picture books, chapter books, comics and magazine pages. He lives in a quiet part of Chennai with his family and books.

Other books in the series:

Gulgul in Jungalu

Gulgul in Sea-saw Gara

The ADVENTURES of Gulgul

GULGUL IN PARA PARA

Ashok Rajagopalan

talking CUB
An Imprint of Speaking Tiger Books

TALKING CUB

Published by Speaking Tiger Books LLP
4381/4, Ansari Road, Daryaganj

New Delhi 110002

First published in paperback in Talking Cub
by Speaking Tiger Books in 2020

ISBN: 978-93-89958-98-0
10 9 8 7 6 5 4 3 2 1

Typeset in Crimson Text by Jojy Philip
Printed At: MP Printers (A unit of DB Corp. Ltd.) Noida 201305

To Sudeshna Shome Ghosh,
friend, philosopher and
editor of this series

Moon Silver

'No?' asked Gulgul sadly.

'NO!' said her father.

'Nowhere?'

'Yes, nowhere,' said Jit. 'We are not going anywhere this time. We are staying in our own planet GR33N. Safe and sound at home.'

Gulgul did not like saying GR33N, so she called her home planet GREEN. That was because the name GR33N looked like 'GREEN' from a distance. And the planet was really green with plenty of plants and trees and grass.

'Why, Papa?' asked Gulgul. 'We had great fun in Jungalu. We had an exciting adventure in Sea-saw Gara.'

'Fun? Adventure? We were stuck in Jungalu with silly animals! And that sinking turtle-island in Sea-saw Gara! Dangerous! Nowhere is where we go this time!'

'And nearly got eaten by merlions, too,' said Megha.

'Mamma! You're not helping!'

'Anyway, your teacher asked you to do something in the holidays,' said Megha. 'Your school assignment. You're supposed to begin collecting something. Shells or stones or something.'

'There's loads of time for that, Mamma,' said Gulgul. 'Nearly two months to re-opening.'

She turned to Paru, her robot parrot.

'Paru! Please ask Papa politely to take us someplace. Last time, Papa listened to you.'

Paru was very good at speaking politely.

'Please, please, Papa...' began Paru.

'Stop that,' said Jit, 'I am not listening to parrots this time, polite or not!'

TRRRRRRRRINGRING! Jit's phone rang.

'Call from Jinny,' announced the phone. Jinny was Jit's sister and Gulgul's aunt.

'What's she calling us for? Wall, take the call,' Jit told the TV wall.

'HIIIIIIIIIIIIIIII! GULGUL! JITTY WITTY! MEGHA

WEGHA!' A jolly face filled the TV wall.

'HEY!' shouted Jit. 'DON'T YELL AT ME, YOU LOUD JIN!'

'DON'T YELL BACK, YOU HORRIBLE BROTHER!' said Jinny.

'Bro and Sis!' said Megha. 'Stop fighting!'

'She yelled first,' said Jit.

'Just a hi. Only said hi! How can someone say "hi" quietly?'

'Hi, Aunt Jinny,' said Gulgul.

'Hi Gulgul. Have great news for you!'

'What, what, what?' asked Gulgul. 'What news, Aunt Jinny?'

'Don't be rude, dear,' said Megha. 'Aunty will tell you.'

'Aunty wishes to invite you to my baby waby's birthday party!' announced Jinny.

'Baby waby?' asked Paru.

'Is it Dee's birthday already?' asked Gulgul. Dee, or Dinny, was Jinny's daughter and Gulgul's cousin.

'Tomorrow,' said Jinny.

'Sorry, Jin, can't come,' said Jit. 'I have loads and loads of work. Can't take a day off. Can't come anywhere. Can go nowhere. So, sorry.'

'I am sorry, too, Jin. I am busy designing a tinkarouty,' said Megha.

Megha was a genius, an engineer and inventor. She was the one who had designed and made Paru for Gulgul.

'So I can't come either. Very sorry! You see, a tinkarouty is an important machine that can repair a car. It can repair cars even in mid-air. When they are flying, I mean. It is something I have been planning to...'

'Whatever,' said Jinny. 'Who asked you two? You're always no-fun busy-wissy people. Just send along my favourite darling niece, Gully-gully.'

'She has a school assignment to do,' Megha replied. 'She hasn't even begun.'

'Oh, I will do that there, Mamma,' said Gulgul. 'I can start collecting something there. Can't I, Aunt Jinny?'

'Of course you can, Gully darling. My Dinny collects feathers. She's got tons of feathers.'

'Oh, then I know just the thing to give Dinny for her birthday!' said Megha. 'It will help her in collecting feathers.'

'And I will come and collect my

niece first thing in the morning,' said Jinny.

'Please collect this poor parrot too,' said Polite Paru.

'Of course, Paru-waru! You too! See ya'll tomorrow! Bye-bye! Bubbbyeeee!'

Aunty Jinny came over the next day to take Gulgul to her house. Jinny's house was on one of the three moons that went round Gulgul's planet. Their moon was named 51LV3R, but Gulgul called it Silver, because the name 51LV3R looked like 'Silver' from a distance.

'SIL-VER!' shouted Gulgul.

'SIL-VER! SIL-VER!
Off to Silver! Yay!'

'We will have a great time! YAY!' said Jinny, dancing around the house with Gulgul.

'Yay! A great day!' said Paru, flying above their heads.

'Whew! Megha and I can look forward to a quiet time here,' said Jit. 'Off you go, you noisy girls.' The noisy three danced all the way to the roof. Jinny had parked her sky racer there. Megha went over to take a look at it.

'Have you checked everything?' she asked Jinny. 'Enough fuel? No loose parts? Solar panels working?'

'Yes, yes, yes! Everything's all right, Megha. Okay, folks, have to leave now. Kids and parents are waiting. Can't stand here chit-chatting.' She pushed Gulgul into the car and took the pilot's seat.

'Here are your things, dear,' said

Megha. She gave her daughter a bag and a big box.

'What is in that box, Mamma?' asked Gulgul.

'That's a little surprise for Little Dinny. Her birthday present.'

'Ooh! Can't wait to see what is inside!'

'Great, thanks,' said Jinny. 'Let's go!' She switched on the engine.

ZOORROOOM!

'A car as noisy as my sister,' said Jit.

VROOOM, ZIPPPP! The car shot into the sky.

Feathers!

'Happy Birthday, Dee dear,' yelled Gulgul, giving her cousin a big hug.

Ten children had come to the party. They ate creamy cake, drank fizzy juice, played noisy games and went 'ooh' and 'aah' over the fun gifts. Tired and sleepy, Gulgul and Dinny went to bed soon after all the guests had gone.

In the morning, Gulgul woke up to her aunt's loud 'GOOOOOOOD MORNEEEEEEEEEEEENGGGGG DARLEEEEEEENGS!'

'Wake up, girls! Have to go! Time to leave!'

'Go? Home?' Gulgul rubbed her eyes. 'So soon, Aunt Jinny? Why?'

'Nooooo! Not your home,' said Dinny, jumping up and down on the bed. 'We are going on holiday!'

'We are going to P4R4P4R4, didn't I tell you?' said Jinny. 'Must have forgotten. A holiday trip. That's my birthday gift to Dinny. We are going there to get a feather.'

'Feather?' asked Gulgul.

'Yes, feather,' said her aunt. 'A keypock's feather.'

'What's a keypock?' asked Gulgul.

'Wait and see,' said Jinny. 'Now get off the bed.'

'But we have to tell Mamma and Papa,' said Gulgul. 'Have to get their permission, don't we?'

'Will do that right now. You go brush your teeth. Will call your Mamma and tell her,' said Jinny. 'Phone, call Mamma.'

'Mamma? Whose Mamma?' asked Jinny's phone. 'Your Mamma? Anybody's Mamma?'

'Call Megha, you stupid phone!' shouted Jinny.

'I am not stupid,' the phone said. 'You weren't clear. Speak slowly and clearly always. Calling Megha.'

TRING TRING. CLICK!

'Hi Jinny,' said Megha.

'Megha, am taking the kids to P4R4P4R4 to get a keypock feather,' said Jinny.

'Keypock? P4R4P4R4? Where's that? Hey, Jit! JIT! Where's P4R4P4R4?'

'Wall!' said Jit to the TV wall. 'Where is P4R4P4R4?'

'Fine, you two have fun finding out,' said Jinny. 'BUBBBYEEEE!'

'HEY, WAIT!' yelled Jit.

'Finding P4R4P4R4,' said the TV wall. 'P4R4P4R4 is a small group of little planets and tiny moons about a zillion kilometres from GR33N.'

'Stop them!' said Jit. 'We can't allow my silly sister to take our dear daughter with her. She's never serious or safe. She's dangerous! She's funny!'

'Wall, call Funny,' said Megha. 'I mean, Jinny. Call Jinny.'

'Calling Jinny,' said the wall.

TRING TRING TRING. Beep!

'Sorry, she is unreachable,' said the wall.

'Keep trying, Wall,' said Megha.

'Trying again. Calling Jinny.'

TRING TRING TRING. Beep! TRING TRING TRING TRING. Beep!

'Sorry, she is unreachable.'

'Oh, what shall we do!' said Jit.

'We have to stop them!' said Megha. 'Wall, call Gulgul!'

'Calling Gulgul.'

TRING TRING TRING TRING.

'TARA TARA, TARA LA LA LA!' said Gulgul's phone from the next room.

'She forgot to take her phone,' said Megha.

'That irresponsible pest!' shouted Jit.

'Oh, what shall we do?' asked Megha. 'We have to stop them.'

Meanwhile, Gulgul and Dinny had finished packing. Jinny went around her space racer, checking everything.

'Fuel full, check,' she said. 'Solar

panels check. Phones check. Batteries check. Trackers check.'

'P4R4P4R4?' said Gulgul. 'Let's call it Parapara. From a distance...'

'The name looks like Parapara,' said Dinny.

'Right!'

'Paru Paru?' said Paru.

'Parapara. Nice name!' said Aunt Jinny. 'Come let's go. It's alright. Told your parents.'

'What's special about Parapara?' asked Gulgul. 'Why go there for feathers?'

'One second,' said Dinny. She ran from the room. She returned with a big book in her hands.

'See, Gulgul,' Dinny opened the book. 'I collect feathers.'

'Yes, Aunty told me you collect feathers,' said Gulgul. The book was an album, full of feathers of all colours, shapes and sizes. Dinny had labelled each feather neatly.

'Yellow crow,' read Gulgul. 'Wow! I have never seen a yellow crow!'

'You can see them here, on Silver,' said Dinny. 'Look at this one that

Mummy got me from your planet. A pretty peacock feather.'

'What's a keypock then?' asked Gulgul. Dinny had a blank page in her album with the label, 'Keypock'.

'It's like a peacock,' said Dinny. 'But, you know, its feathers change colours. All the colours of the rainbow, one by one.'

'Wow!'

Aunt Jinny grabbed the album and snapped it shut.

'Come, come,' she said, 'Time to go! You can talk about feathers in the car. If we start now, we will reach Parapara by noon.'

'Wait, Mummy,' said Dinny. 'I haven't opened Aunt Megha's present yet. I forgot!'

'It's still in the car. In the dicky wicky. You can open it on the way, let's go.'

'Also my binocap! Wait, Mummy!' said Dinny, dashing back to her room.

'Hmmph!' grumbled her mother. 'I hate to wait!'

The Squawkatoo

'It will take us an hour to reach Parapara,' announced Jinny. The car sped through black space towards the little stars far away.

'Awwwww!' said Dinny, opening Megha's gift box.

'What is it?' asked Gulgul. 'What? What? What?'

In the box was a toy bird on a stand. On the stand was a label that said, 'Squawkatoo'.

Dinny clapped her hands in delight.

'What's a squawkatoo?' asked her mother.

'I don't know, Mummy. But it's cute. Has a funny name, too!'

'I know, I remember,' said Gulgul. 'I have seen Mamma make this. It translates anything we say into bird language and back. That's why she thought you will find it useful. To ask birds for their feathers, you know.'

'Oh, how useful. I have the best aunt in the universe,' said Dinny, jumping up and down in her seat.

'Don't rock the car, Baby waby,' said her mother.

'Let's see how it works,' said Gulgul. She pressed the button on the toy's stand.

'Hi, pretty keypock.'

'Twee! Twitty twee squawk,' said the squawkatoo.

'Yay!' yelled the two girls.

'We have arrived,' said Jinny as she slowed down the space-car. 'This is Parapara.'

'Wow, look at that,' said Gulgul.

Their car had just entered the group of planets called P4R4P4R4. P4R4P4R4 had more than a hundred planets of various sizes. The smaller ones were only as big as Gulgul's school. Their moons were just giant balls, about the size of her house. The biggest planet of them all was only the size of a city.

'Here,' Dinny gave Gulgul her binocap. 'Look through this.'

'Wow! So many birds!' said Gulgul. Birds were everywhere. They flew here and there, cooing, cawing, crowing, quacking, squawking and singing.

'Too much noise,' said Jinny.

'Lots of feathers,' laughed Dinny.

'Paru has no feathers,' said the parrot sadly.

'Have to find out where the keypocks live,' said Jinny. 'Let's land on that big planet there and ask somebody.' She pointed to the biggest of the planets. She steered the car carefully around the planets and moons and birds in the way.

The big planet was wholly covered by giant trees. Nothing but trunks and branches and leaves could be seen. No space in between the trees. No grass or mud or sand could be seen.

'This planet is greener than our Green,' declared Gulgul.

'AAAAARGH! No place to land! Help!' said Jinny.

'What should we do?'

'Even if there is a lake, pond or river, it will do,' said Jinny. 'This car can float on water.' But no pond or lake could be seen below.

'Look, Aunt Jinny,' Gulgul, looking through the binocap, pointed to a tree. Atop the tree was what appeared to be a broad and flat bed of feathers.

'Can we land on that?' asked Gulgul. 'There seems to be more than enough space for our car.'

'Okay, let's do that. There's nowhere else, anyway.' The car slowly and carefully dipped. Down it went, towards the bed.

SQUAWK! QUACK! **CAW!** COO! **TWITTER,** FLUTTER, **FLAP** FLAP **FLAP!**

A flurry of furious birds, big and small, flew out of their way in a hurry. It was not a bed of feathers they had landed on. It was a great flock of birds on a platform of wood!

'Oops!' said Jinny. The angry birds screeched and returned to the platform. They gathered around the car. Some pecked at it. Others

screeched at them, flapping their wings.

PECK, PECK, PECK. PATACK! TINKLE! PLINK, PLINK.

'They have broken our headlights!' shouted Jinny.

'Rude birdies,' said Paru.

'What do we do?' asked Dinny.

'It's not safe to get out of the car,' said her mother. 'We have to take off. We have to go back.'

'Return home? Awww, Mummy!' Dinny looked sadly at all the feathers flying around.

'Sorry, my Baby waby!' Jinny raced the engine. 'Will think of something else to give you for your birthday. We have to leave before they peck our car into pieces!'

Par King Place

'Wait, wait, Aunt Jinny,' said Gulgul, 'Let's not leave yet. They have stopped attacking us.'

An old fluffy bird had screeched and hissed at the flock of pecking birds and chased them away. It came over to the car and with its beak, knocked gently on the glass top.

'It's asking us to open up,' said Gulgul.

'Hope it's safe to do that,' said Jinny. 'Okay, here goes...'

She pushed the button to open the top.

'Ugghhh!' Jinny held her nose. 'What a stink!'

'Yes,' said Gulgul, 'Strong birdie smell.'

'Aaah,' said Dinny, 'The sweet smell of feathers!'

'Twoo Squa woo? Twirrr arrrr wooo prummm?' asked the fluffy bird.

'What's it saying?' asked Jinny.

'Let's use the squawkatoo, Mummy!'

'Good idea, Dee, take it out, quickly.'

Dinny took the toy bird out and pressed its switch.

'Twoo Squa woo? Twere arrrr wooo prummm?' asked the fluffy bird again.

'Who are you? Where are you from?' said the toy bird.

'We are humans from a planet far away. We are sorry that we landed here. Big mistake,' Jinny replied.

The squawkatoo tweeted and squawked the reply to the fluffy bird.

The fluffy bird stared at them in silence for a while, and then spoke.

'Twilcoo too Tweenpara, yuyu! Yumyum Win King Beebee.'

'Welcome to Greenpara, humans! I am Win King Bird,' translated the squawkatoo.

'Ask him if he's the king of the

birds here, Squawkatoo,' said Jinny. The squawkatoo squawked.

'Maybe the biggest bird is king here,' said Gulgul. 'He seems to be the biggest bird here.'

Win King did not reply. It just stood there and blinked. Then it pointed to four birds behind him.

'They are Thin King, Blin King and Coo King, Win King says,' said the toy bird.

'What are they thinking, blinking or cooking?' asked Paru.

'Ha ha ha,' laughed Gulgul.

'What funny names!'

The toy bird translated that: 'Squawk twunny tways!'

That upset the three King birds.

'Somebody switch off the squawkatoo,' said Jinny. 'It's translating everything we say.'

'They are all kings here,' said Dinny, switching off the squawkatoo.

'Why no queens?' asked Jinny. 'I don't like this. Where are the ladies?'

Dinny switched on the squawkatoo.

'Twi noo tweens? Twere twa twee la-la-lees?' it asked.

That question made Win King mad. It squawked and squeaked in their ears. Jinny and the girls stepped back, scared.

'There are no kings or queens here,' explained the squawkatoo. 'All are equal. And Win King is a lady, not a gentle-bird, she says. Thin King is her daughter. Blin King and Coo King are her boys.'

'Oops, sorry, Madam,' said Jinny.

'Ooh! I understand. "King" is just part of their names,' said Dinny. 'Pleased to meet y'all! Ow! Aah!'

Coo King had plucked off a strand of Dinny's hair. Then he gave her one of his feathers.

'Oooh! Aaah!' said Gulgul.

'Ow! Ouchy!' said Aunt Jinny. The other two birds had taken hair and given them feathers in return.

'This is how they greet each other here,' explained the toy bird.

'How painful,' said Gulgul, with

watery eyes. Her aunt and cousin had tears in their eyes, too.

'At least we got a few feathers,' said Dinny.

'Let's not meet and greet more birds then,' said Aunt Jinny. 'Let's just collect fallen feathers and head home.'

Then Win King invited the three to her home.

'Ooh!' said Gulgul. 'A bird house! Let's go, Aunt Jinny.'

Leaving the space-car on the platform, the three flew to the bird house on the backs of Thin King, Blin King and Coo King. Win King led the way.

The King house was one of the tallest trees on the planet. It was decorated with creeper curtains and sweet-smelling flowers.

'Wow,' said Gulgul. 'It's not an itty-bitty bird house: it's a bird palace!'

'Welcome to Par King Place,' said Win King, as the birds dropped to a big broad branch.

'Please take care of your guests, children,' she said and flew into a large hole in the trunk of the tree house.

'Please perch anywhere you like,' said Coo King. He pointed to a row of round beds of dried leaves.

'Would you like to drink some yummy worm juice?' asked Blin King.

'No, thank you, Blin King,' said the three humans at the same time.

'Fruit? Please eat some fruit, then,' begged Thin King.

'Yes, thank you, Thin King,' chorused the humans.

'Nice and sweet King family,' said Gulgul.

'Yes! Just like this fruit!' said Dinny, biting into a big yellow fruit.

Fighter Pocks

'It's nice and comfy here.' Gulgul leaned back on her bed of leaves and closed her eyes.

'Yes,' said Dinny. 'But we need to go see a keypock and collect a feather or two. Where do the keypocks live?'

'Let me ask a King kid. Switch on the squawkatoo, Dinny.'

Dinny had switched off the toy bird to save its battery power.

'Oh, Coo King, where do we find keypocks?' asked Gulgul.

'O Coo Kwee, twere too twee fee keepoo?' the squawkatoo asked Coo King.

'SQUAWK!' cried the three King kids and flew away from the branch.

'What now?' asked Aunt Jinny. 'Why did they fly off?'

'Let's ask them,' said Gulgul. The birds were now on a branch above.

'Ask them why they flew off,' Gulgul told the squawkatoo. The squawkatoo squawked but Thin King and Blin King did not reply.

Finally, Coo King said, 'We are afraid of those birds. They are proud and fierce birds. They get angry easily. They fight and peck with sharp beaks and claws. They are not peace pocks. They are fighter pocks!'

'Oooh,' said Dinny.

'Okay, let's go home,' said Jinny. 'Baby waby, I'll get you another gift. I may get you the fine feather of a mynah or a mayjah.'

'That we can get anytime from

Gulgul's planet, Mummy,' said Dinny. 'I need a keypock's feather! I told all my friends that I'll get one!'

'Maybe the keypock's only scary to these King birds,' said Gulgul. 'Maybe they will be nice and sweet to us.'

'Hmm, maybe,' said her aunt.

'Where do they live?' Gulgul asked the squawkatoo to ask Coo King.

'In Pockapara,' said Coo King.

'Will you take us there, please?' asked Jinny.

'What? NO!'

'N o o o o o o o o o o o o o o o o o o!' shouted Thin King.

'Never!' shrieked Blin King.

'What do we do?' asked Dinny.

'Will you take us to our car, please?' asked Gulgul.

'Pease, please, pretty birdies,' said Paru.

'We'll have to ask Mother,' said Blin King.

Win King gave them permission after Paru asked

her politely. Nobody could say 'No' to the polite parrot.

The King kids flew the humans back to their car and returned to Par King Place. The sky had grown dark by the time they reached the platform. Their car still stood there, in the midst of a gathering of curious birds.

'How quickly it's grown dark,' said Dinny.

'Since this is a small planet, days and nights are shorter than in Green,' explained Jinny.

'I'm glad I don't live here!'

'I won't mind living here,' said Dinny. 'Feathers. Days and nights can be short, as long as the feathers are long.'

'You and your feathers,' laughed Gulgul.

'Okay, let's move,' said Jinny. 'Get in, darlings.'

ZOORROOOM!

'The headlights don't work,' said Jinny. 'These nasty birds have broken our headlights!'

'Bad Birdies,' scolded Paru.

'Won't these do?' asked Gulgul, taking two torchlights from her bag. 'Dinny and I can hold them up while you drive.'

'That's a good idea for outer space,' said her aunt. 'But I wouldn't risk flying without proper headlights through these trees. Those branches will break my car in two.'

'Then, let's wait for day, Aunt Jinny. Luckily, we don't have to wait long here.'

'I'll collect some feathers while we wait,' said Dinny, getting out of the

car. 'Coming, Gulgul? You can start collecting feathers, too.'

Finding Pockapara

A few hours and fine feathers later, the three took off.

'Now, where do we go?' asked Jinny. 'There are so many planets here. Which is the keypock one?' She had flown the car around Parapara for an hour.

'The car map does not show the names of planets here.'

'Oh, what do we do now?' asked Dinny.

'Can Paru help?' asked Paru.

'Oh, yes, I know!' said Gulgul. 'Paru can help. Aunt Jinny, let's land somewhere. I think I have an idea.'

Jinny landed the car on a little moon, which was really just a big rock.

'Whew!' said Jinny. 'I can sure use some rest.'

'How may Paru be of help?' asked Paru.

'She can find out where Pockapara is. She can fly about and ask the birds.'

'But she can't speak their language. How can she make them understand?'

'Oh she can learn that from the squawkatoo,' said Gulgul. 'She is a fast learner, aren't you, Paru?'

'Paru learns things fast,' said Paru proudly.

'Good idea, Gulgul.' Dinny took out the toy bird and said:

'Where is Pockapara? How do I go there?'

'Twere ee Pockapara? Towoo too hi toe twere?' translated the toy bird.

'Wonderful!' said Gulgul. 'Now, Paru, learn those lines.'

Paru learnt the lines in no time. Then Gulgul sent her off in search of the planet of keypocks.

'Bye, Paru!' she said. 'Come back with the location of Pockapara!'

'Bye, Paru will be back,' said Paru and flew away.

'No feathers here,' said Dinny. 'Or I could have collected some while waiting.'

'You have lots already,' said her mother. 'Too much! We don't have space inside the car for more. Still more feathers, and we would have to stick them all over the car.'

'Ha ha ha,' laughed Gulgul. 'We will look like a Parapara bird ourselves then.'

'Ha ha ha,' laughed Dinny.

'We go to this keypock place, collect the keypock feather, and go home,' said Jinny. 'That's the plan.'

'We can use my torches for headlights,' said Gulgul, taking them out again.

'Yes, we have to,' said her aunt.

'Here comes Paru,' said Dinny.

'Yay!' said Gulgul. 'Welcome back, my sweet pet!'

'Did you find the Porapacka place, Paru-waru?' asked Jinny.

'Pockapara, Mummy,' Dinny corrected her.

'Whatever! Well, Paru? Do you know the way?'

'Paru will show you the way,' said the parrot.

'Yay!' yelled Gulgul and Dinny.

They got into the car and Vroom! The space-car shot into the sky. Paru flew in front to show the way. Gulgul and Dinny held up the torches.

'Can't Paru-waru fly any faster?' asked Jinny, slowing down to match the parrot's speed.

'Mummy!' said Dinny. 'She's only a poor little parrot!'

'But she's a poor little robotic parrot! Wish Megha had made her fly faster.'

'Will ask Mamma if she can,' promised Gulgul.

They flew past a few planets and moons, turned right at Greenpara, then straight to the other end of Parapara.

'We had been driving around in the wrong direction,' said Jinny. 'If those silly scaredy Thin King, Blin King and Bay King birds had helped us, we would have saved a lot of time.'

'Coo King, not Bay King, Mummy,' said Dinny.

'Whatever!'

Chum Key

'Wow! See the glowing lights!' pointed Gulgul.

Planet Pockapara's night side was dotted with hundreds of little lights.

'Just like our planet,' said Gulgul. 'There are buildings here, then.'

'Whew,' said her aunt. 'Buildings are what I wish to see. I'm sick and tired of trees and leaves and feathers.'

'Awww, Mummy!' said Dinny.

'Let's not land on the night side of the planet. Tough to land there,' said Jinny. 'Let's go over to the day side where it's morning. That will give us enough time to look for the keypocky birdies.'

Jinny flew the car around the planet, over to its day side.

'More trees! No buildings!' complained Jinny, staring at the land below.

'But, look, Aunt Jinny,' said Gulgul, 'Lots of land and grass and all.'

Sure enough, the planet was not completely covered by trees but had grassy gaps and a choice of space to land.

Jinny brought her space-car down to a stretch of grass. White and violet wild flowers bloomed; bushes with

blue leaves and yellow fruit grew all around.

'What a pretty place,' said Dinny.

'Smells nice and sweet, too,' said Gulgul.

'Let's go look for the funny feathered birdies now,' said Jinny. 'YOOHOO, KEYPOCKIES, WHERE ARE YOU!'

'Mummy! Let's go look! No need to yell for them. Rudely, too! We don't want to make them mad at us.'

'Hmmmph! Okay, let's go over to those trees. Appears to be a forest. That's where we are most likely to find them.' Jinny pointed to a group of trees close by.

The three walked over to the trees, followed by Paru.

'Oh oopsy!' said Dinny. 'We forgot the squawkatoo.'

'You two keep walking,' said Gulgul. 'I will go get the squawkatoo.'

She ran back towards the car.

Gulgul soon dashed back with the toy bird. But she couldn't see her aunt or cousin anywhere near the trees.

'Aunt Jinny? Dinny?' she called out. 'Where are you?'

There was no answer. Worried, Gulgul walked further, into the forest.

'Twee twee twee!' said a voice from behind a bush.

'What's that? Who's there?' Gulgul ran to look behind the bush.

'Twee tee,' cried a bird. It was about

the size of a hen, but its feathers were silver in colour, shining like little mirrors in the sunlight.

'Oh you poor thing,' said Gulgul. 'Why do you cry?'

'Twee tee,' replied the bird.

'Oh, I am a stupid thing,' Gulgul switched on the squawkatoo.

'Help me!' said the silver bird.

'Of course I will,' said Gulgul. 'What happened?'

'I hurt my wing,' the bird lifted its right wing to show where some feathers were missing.

'Oh, where's your nest?'

'It's too far to walk. I have very short legs, you see.'

'Hmm,' said Gulgul. 'Hop on to my shoulder, and I will take you there.'

'Thank you!' The bird hopped on to Gulgul's shoulder.

'You are a cute bird. What's your name? I am Gulgul. Owww!'

The bird had bitten off a strand

of Gulgul's hair. It gave her a silver feather in return.

'I am Chum Key,' it said. 'Please turn left at that tree.'

Gulgul turned left, then right, till they came to a thick circle of round bushes around a mound. On the mound was a big fat tree.

'Careful here,' said Chum Key.

'Why? Why be careful?' asked Gulgul.

'Big bad birds live here. Don't make any noise while you pass that tree.'

'Gully gully!'

'Paru!' said Gulgul. The parrot had flown down from the tree.

'What are you doing here?' asked Gulgul. 'Where are the others?'

'Up the tree,' said Paru.

'But how did they get there? How do I go there?'

'Don't! Danger! Big bad birds!' Chum Key jumped around.

'But my people are up there. What do we do, Paru?'

'And watch out for that net!' squeaked Chum Key.

'Net? What net?' HOOOOOO… OOOOOOOSH! A mesh of vines and creepers scooped them up and pulled them up in the air.

'HELP!' yelled Gulgul.

Caged!

'Where are we?' asked Gulgul. 'What's happening? Who did this? Why? How?'

Her questions were soon answered. A big parrot, nearly the size of a horse, pulled them up to a branch. Seeing its catch, it screeched and clapped its wings in delight.

'What's it saying?' Gulgul asked the squawkatoo.

'See what I caught, Ma! May I keep them?' it explained.

A voice answered from a hole in the trunk of the tree.

'You have too many pets, already, dear. We don't have enough space. And who will feed and clean them?'

'Awww, Ma,' said the parrot. 'The cage you made for me is big enough for more. I promise to take care of them.'

Hopping to another branch with the net, the parrot dumped Gulgul

and Chum Key into a dark cage made of wooden sticks.

'Tweet, twitter, me twits, twitty too!' said the parrot as she locked the door to the cage.

The toy bird translated, 'Have fun, my pets. Love you!'

'I don't like being a pet!' yelled Gulgul.

'Neither do we,' said two voices from the back of the cage.

'Aunt Jinny! Dinny!' said Gulgul. Dinny ran over to Gulgul and hugged her tightly.

'We were captured by this horrible bird, too,' said Jinny.

'Didn't even give me its feather,' complained Dinny.

'Paru's not like this bad parrot,' said Paru. 'Paru's a good parrot.'

'And I don't keep Paru in a cage,' said Gulgul.

'Twy Tweet twittee twee twit too!' chimed Chum Key.

'I hate being a pet, too,' translated the toy bird.

'Who's that birdie?' asked Jinny.

'Oops!' said Gulgul. 'Forgot my manners. Chum Key, this is my aunt Jinny and cousin Dinny. Aunt Jinny, Dee, this is Chum Key. She's hurt her wing and I was taking her to her nest.'

The squawkatoo twitted and

tweeted the introduction to Chum Key.

Chum Key gave Jinny and Dinny feathers after biting off bits of their hair.

'Ow! Pleased to meet ya,' said Dinny.

'Ouch!' said Jinny. 'The sooner I go home the better. Or I will forget to shake hands and start plucking people's hair!'

'Okay, now what do we do?' asked Dinny. 'We are stuck here.'

It soon grew dark. Inside the cage, it became darker.

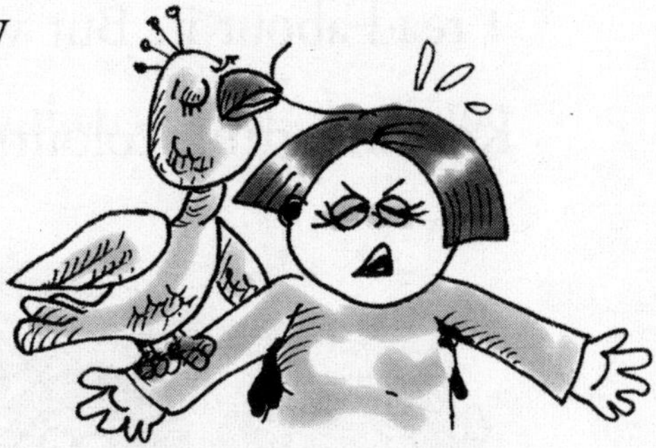

Nothing could be seen.

Suddenly, the cage was lit by a soft light.

'Ooh!' said Dinny. 'Look!'

'Oooooh!' said Gulgul.

Chum Key glowed in the dark like a table lamp. Her feathers shone like little lights.

'She's a little keypock!' said Dinny. 'I read about it. But why isn't Chum Key changing colours?'

'Let's ask her,' said Gulgul. 'Squawkatoo, ask her why she's not changing colours.'

'Only big keypocks can change colours,' explained Chum Key. 'They can shine brighter, too. I am only a key-chick.'

'What's that?' asked Dinny, pointing to the sky where two bright lights floated about.

'Is it a plane? Is it a car?' asked Jinny.

'It's not a plane, it's a bird! Two birds, actually,' said Gulgul, looking through the binocap.

'TWITEEEEEEEEEEE!' screamed Chum Key.

'MUMMMEEEE!' translated the squawkatoo.

Attack of the Keypocks

'Keypocks!' said Dinny. 'Two big keypocks!'

The pair of keypocks shone brightly in the night. They were like two big yellow lights. Soon, they turned orange, then red. They swooped down to the branch with the cage.

'Twitteeee!' cried Chum Key.

'Chum Key!' cried her parents.

'Twitty too?' asked the big parrot, who had come there just then.

'Twee twittee squawk twere!' complained Chum Key.

The red keypocks appeared to be very angry. They screeched and squawked and pecked at the parrot till it said, 'Tworeee!'

'Sorry!' translated the squawkatoo.

'That will teach her not to keep us caged like this,' said Gulgul.

Mamma Keypock pecked at the cage till it broke open.

'Whew!' said Jinny, coming out of the cage.

'What's "thank you", Squawkatoo?' asked Gulgul.

'Twattoo!' said the toy bird. 'Twattoo, Keypocks!'

Chum Key told her parents how Gulgul had helped her.

The big keypocks changed colour from angry red to purple to a happy blue. They were no longer angry now. Mamma Keypock hugged them all with her blue wing.

'Twall lof twoo twee tum too twour nee!' she said.

The toy bird explained that the keypock was inviting everybody to her nest.

The keypocks lived atop a rocky hill in a cool cave. Keypock feathers of all colours covered the floor.

'Beautiful!' said Dinny. 'What pretty feathers!'

'May we have some?' asked Gulgul. Chum Key gave the girls about a dozen keypock feathers.

'Yay!' Dinny danced around holding them. 'We are rich.'

'Twattoo, Chum Key,' said Gulgul.

'Okay, time to go home,' Jinny told them. They had eaten some fruit and drank water. It was morning now in Pockapara.

'Squawkatoo,' said Gulgul, 'please

ask the keypocks to take us to our space-car.'

Gulgul and Dinny hugged Chum Key goodbye. The key-chick could not fly yet, with her broken wing. Mamma Keypock picked up the two girls and flew, followed by Papa Keypock with Jinny. Paru led the way to the car.

'There's our car,' Gulgul spotted it in the grass below.

'Look,' said Dinny, 'There's another car next to it.'

The keypocks who were blue,

turned green, then yellow, orange, and finally red.

Dropping the girls and Jinny safely on the ground, they dashed towards the new car.

They began pecking it all over.

PECK,

PECK,

PECK.

PATACK!

TINKLE!

PLINK,

PLINK.

They broke the headlights.

'Hey, wait! Stop!' shouted Gulgul. 'That's my Mamma's car!'

'Let's stop them!'

'Squawkatoo,' said Gulgul. 'Ask

them to stop attacking the car. Tell them that they are my parents.'

Running towards the angry keypocks with the toy bird held high, Gulgul managed to stop the attack.

Finally, after the keypocks had flown away, Megha and Jit came out of their car.

'Mamma, Papa!' Gulgul hugged them. 'What are you doing here?'

'Searching for our daughter, what else,' said Jit. 'Whew! Those keypocks sure are scary birds.'

'No, Uncle Jit,' said Dinny, 'They

are sweet. See, they gave us lots of feathers.'

'They gave us quite a scare!' said Megha. 'They have broken our headlights.'

'We went all over Parapara looking for you,' Jit told Jinny. 'Jin, shame on you! You bad sister! You irresponsible aunt! You did not wait to get my permission to take Gulgul to such places. Dangerous places!'

'As if you never took her to dangerous places,' shouted back Jinny. 'What about that Jungalu place? How about that watery place with merlions and stuff?'

'Bro and Sis, stop fighting,' said Megha. 'Let's all leave this place now.'

'But we don't have lights!' yelled Jit. 'Those horrible birds have broken our headlights.'

'We used my torches for Aunt Jinny's car,' said Gulgul proudly. 'My idea!'

'We don't have any torches,' said Megha. 'What do we do?'

'We will be fined by the space police,' said Jit.

'I have an idea!' said Gulgul.

Feather Lights

The two space-cars took off soon after, thanks to Gulgul's idea.

'Look, Dee,' said Gulgul, as their car flew around to the night side of Pockapara. 'Those lights we saw when we came were not buildings.'

'No, Gulgul, they were keypocks.'

'A very bright idea, ha ha!' said Megha, as she steered the car carefully around the small planets and tiny moons of Parapara.

Gulgul's idea was to fix two keypock feathers on each car.

'A brilliant idea. They shine brighter than our headlights,' said Megha, proud of her daughter.

'I wish they didn't keep changing colours though,' complained Jit. 'People in other cars are laughing at us.'

'Better colour-changing lights than no lights at all,' said Megha.

'Why is Gulgul not with us?' asked Jit. 'We could have taken her home with us, and they could have gone to Silver.'

'Gulgul's staying with them for two days,' explained Megha. 'Dinny's helping her with her feather collection.'

'Did you tell my funny sister not to take my daughter out to any more places?' asked Jit.

'Oh, Jinny is sick and tired of travelling. She's not going anywhere. She says she's going to stay in bed for a week.'

'That's safe, not only for her, but for all.'

Meanwhile, in Jinny's car, the girls had a great time looking at the feathers they had gathered.

'I have about a dozen feathers,' Gulgul told Dinny. 'Hope my teacher thinks it's enough for a collection.'

'Oh, don't worry, Gulgul. I will give you my doubles and triples.'

'What are doubles and triples?' asked her mother.

'Two of the same make a double,' explained Dinny. 'Three's triple.

When kids collect things, we keep these doubles for exchange. You know, a friend will have two of what I don't and...'

'Okay, fine, whatever! I am sorry I asked.'

'Thank you, Dee,' said Gulgul. 'With your doubles, I will have double the number of feathers I have now.'

'You may even have triple that,' said Dinny. 'I have so many doubles!'

'Paru doesn't have a single feather,' said Paru sadly.

'Oh, my album is your album, Paru,' Gulgul told her. 'Gulgul and Paru have lots of feathers.'

'Thank you, kind Gulgul!'

ALSO IN THIS SERIES BY ASHOK RAJAGOPALAN

GULGUL IN JUNGALU

'I am Hatch Patch. Welcome to our blue and green planet. Nice of you to "drop" in! You really dropped in!' The creature laughed at his own joke.

Gulgul is a little girl who lives on the planet GR33N with her parents Jit and Megha. On their way back from a fun day on the planet H4H4H0, their space-car crashes into an unknown lake! They have landed on Jungalu. Here they are rescued by the strange elephant-like Patches and given yummy fruit and grass to eat. But how will they repair their car and return to their own planet? Only Jungalu's Wise Leader, Mahali, the giant mouse, can help them.

Will Megha be able to build her zingjuck that will shoot them back into space? Will the weird and caring animals of Jungalu—the long fellows, bluglugs, flippots and others help them?

Find out in the first adventure story about the clever and naughty girl Gulgul. Ashok Rajagopalan, creator of the bestselling Gajapati Kulapati books, brings his trademark wacky humour to a new series filled with adventure, friendship and fun.

ALSO IN THIS SERIES BY ASHOK RAJAGOPALAN

GULGUL IN SEA-SAW GARA

In the sea, riding the waves was a fleet of five animals that were half-horse and half-fish.
'They are striped,' said Gulgul. 'They are not sea horses. They are seabras!'

Gulgul, along with her parents Megha and Jit, have gone to the planet C-54G4R4, or Sea-saw Gara. The whole planet is a like a giant waterpark. When Gulgul goes on a submarine ride, the submarine loses its way in the planet's waters! Soon they are rescued by giant octopuses who live in Octopus City. Here everyone lives in aquariums and eats sea-fruits, sea-nuts, seagrass, and even drinks seawater!

How will Gulgul and the other humans survive? Will they be able to find their way back to the waterpark? What will happen if the fierce half-fish and half-lion merlions attack?

Laugh out loud as Gulgul once again proves that with a little bit of luck and lots of clever ideas, there are amazing adventures waiting on every planet! Ashok Rajagopalan, creator of the bestselling Gajapati Kulapati books, brings his trademark wacky humour to a new series filled with adventure, friendship and fun.